An Eternity of Nothing

Shanaya Stephens

Ukiyoto Publishing

All global publishing rights are held by

Ukiyoto Publishing

Published in 2025

Content Copyright © Shanaya Stephens

ISBN 9789370099340

All rights reserved.
No part of this publication may be reproduced,
transmitted, or stored in a retrieval system, in any
form by any means, electronic, mechanical,
photocopying, recording or otherwise, without the
prior permission of the publisher.

The moral rights of the authors have been asserted.

This is a work of fiction. Names, characters, businesses,
places, events, locales, and incidents are either the
products of the author's imagination or used in a
fictitious manner. Any resemblance to actual persons,
living or dead, or actual events is purely coincidental.

This book is sold subject to the condition that it shall
not by way of trade or otherwise, be lent, resold, hired
out or otherwise circulated, without the publisher's
prior consent, in any form of binding or cover other
than that in which it is published.

www.ukiyoto.com

Disclaimer

This book is a work of fiction. Any resemblances between any person, place, community, entity, cult, country, or religion are purely coincidental. It doesn't aim to condemn, or harm the beliefs of any community, culture, sect, cult, or religion.

Trigger Warning: <u>NOT ADVISED FOR PEOPLE UNDER 18 YEARS OF AGE</u>

This book contains graphic and disturbing content, including suicide, sexual assault, self-harm, domestic violence, childhood abuse, and predatory behaviour over the internet. These themes are portrayed in a realistic and raw manner, and may be triggering for some readers.

Reader discretion is advised. If you are sensitive to these topics or have experienced trauma related to them, please proceed with caution. This book may not be suitable for all audiences, particularly children and young adults.

The author and publisher acknowledge the sensitive nature of these topics and have made every effort to handle them with respect and care. However, we recognize that reading about these themes can be distressing and potentially triggering.

If you are experiencing distress or need support, please reach out to a trusted adult, mental health professional, or call a helpline such as the National Suicide Prevention Lifeline (1-800-273-TALK (8255) in the US) or a local crisis centre.

Remember, your well-being and safety are important. Please prioritize them when reading this book.

To the Wars we have always lost to

"I am the unlucky lover. I cannot give myself to you. And I cannot go back to myself."

-Mahmoud Darwish

Contents

We are all going to die	1
The Lullaby	6
Asma Fatima	9
Dua	13
An Eternity of Nothing	18
About the author	22
Other Titles by the Author	23

We are all going to die

It was a day in forever, etched in anything but happiness. War planes climbed our skies and threatened to tear the Sun away underneath all those dust clouds. In between we stood there. And in between rested all of what we knew about life.

You must think that peace is what sustains life. I thought so too. But when you see that what keeps the world going is not the silent hum of a morning, but the warm blood of a Turkey's snapped head; sometimes marinated in salt and spices. Sometimes it's not a turkey. Only a human. But it leaves more room for life. All other sorts of life.

I scooped the uncooked, pasty ginger out of the meat. I had never eaten anything that wasn't a vegetable before. Or a cake. Cakes are just so cool. There's nothing that can ever go wrong with a cake. The turkey, however, had one too many flaws. One of the many must be the fact that it moves and makes all those sounds from its weirdly long neck. It's a bird.

An Eternity of Nothing

Birds fly. Birds go somewhere they can be safe, but not Turkeys. And not chickens. And not crows. Especially not the crows. The crows loom around trying to scrape an eye out of a fresh kill. So many eyes for dinner at the feast tonight! They bring their inmates. Sometimes it feels like they too are fighting. The vultures and the crows. The crows and the eagles. The eagles and the owls. It's the absence of this peace that keeps them alive.

"How long before we can go back home?" I ask Asma Fatima, who hasn't once lifted her niqab ever since I have met her. She doesn't answer. Ali sits close to her as she feeds him with her hands. They are all grownups. Though with Ali's long beard it's hard to tell if he was ever young. Asma Fatima holds their baby in her lap. Its head dips in the fold of her niqab as he suckles onto his meal. I was taught it was rude to stare when babies eat. I am not sure if they teach the crows the same. They seemed to have watched for so long, for a moment I thought that the city was going to be invaded by a fleet of them. Thick and fat crows who will feed on everything that couldn't breathe.

This wasn't a good thing to think about. The Turkey's head had hardly started to look appetizing. The knife that bit into his cooked flesh was laced with something yellow and then something red. It swirled out into the bowl and the spices floated to its surface, painting it the yellow of turmeric. Asma Fatima didn't cook well. Or anything else. She has been chopping anything she could set her eyes on. Anything that's not human.

When the war planes move too far, the baby starts crying. It's Asma Fatima's fault. The baby was born only a week ago, right between the planes and crows. When it's slimy head invaginated between her thighs, Ali had held her hand. The Angels had pulled the baby out. There was no way Asma Fatima could do it alone. In its gracious entrance to the world, the baby had nothing less than the grandeur of a royal prince. The sky erupted into trinkets of flame, dancing about the sky as they bombed the camps. The crows cawed in unison. The baby thought it was a sign from the God above. So, it cried for what seemed like the first time. It cried a lot to the sound of the planes. And, let it be known that the baby was special. While Ali had already lost his ear, and Asma Fatima was still searching for a blade to cut off the umbilical cord, it was only when the baby cried that everyone around the camp burst into tears.

Everything started with the baby. The women started running as far as their feet could carry them. Their children followed close behind. Their husbands hadn't been home. Only Ali. If it weren't for the baby, Ali would've left long ago. He told Asma Fatima, long ago. He chided her for it. Even called the baby wretched. But the baby wasn't wretched. The baby was strong. It held my finger so tight, that when the shrapnel came, I could hardly cry when it got my eye. Although blind, and wailing there was little I could do. I put the baby in my lap. Asma Fatima then cut the cord with the shrapnel. It was war that had borne them this little piece of heaven. If it weren't for the baby, we would have moved an inch and died right there.

Asma Fatima had learnt to close her thighs now. It was hard to tell if it was her own blood that marred her skirt. The baby had learnt to recognise the whirring of the planes for his lullaby. Ali turned a little within himself and didn't force Asma Fatima to open her thighs. Some days, even when he threatened to do so. And I thought I couldn't leave when I had already lost an eye. So, we were all here.

The rest of the camp burnt and died. But the baby and us, we survived. We managed to get our food from the catacombs and even though Asma Fatima (as feeble and weak and bad at cooking) thought we would die, we didn't.

The Lullaby

The last of the planes touched the afternoon sky. I asked Ali how he can be so sure, and he shakes his head and speaks in the way only old, lost men can, "I can feel it in my heart, Zubaida," and closes his eyes. Sometimes I think he only does that because he doesn't know anything about the world and how it works. For instance, my name isn't Zubaida. I am too White, and too selfish to have a beautiful name. Also, it's just something that slips easy on his tongue. He told me so.

"Take the name," he insisted, as I sat with one blind eye. "I don't know you, but you must be called Zubaida," a state of urgency possessed him. It was even greater than when he had seen his baby come out to the world.

"But that's not my name," I argued. I had a better name.

"This isn't your country either. You can take it. It's my mother's name. Your people came for my mother land, it's only fair if you take my mother's name," he smiled in a madly allure.

This was what made me stick to Ali. Ali didn't seem like someone you would see hiding in war camps. He carried himself like a Bedouin. And his hands were coarse. Yet, he knew nothing about what went out in the world. This was probably why he married Asma Fatima. She looked like she could age backwards and still know what to do with life. The only thing common between the two was the baby and the helplessness of war. A sense of loss in both of them.

"Will the baby cry then?" I asked Asma Fatima. Now that the war is over there won't be any more planes. It's what I knew. And I knew better than Ali. Even without knowing much about the world. Also, they announced it over the radio. The war planes had rained death on the last surviving camps. The crows populated the tents. The sky was going to fall silent. The sun was ready to make a comeback. The baby, was unprepared. It hadn't known peace. Or fulfilment. Neither had I. Asma Fatima seemed to have been the smartest of us four. She didn't grace me with an answer again. She knew when to save her strength.

"Don't worry about the baby," Ali tells me. That's what he chants every time the light goes out. The nights aren't awfully cold. Something close by is still burning, and is still on fire. Ali chuckles and says, "Pay heed, Zubaida! This is our hearts they burnt. This our lands they burnt. It will always be this warm and searing." He doesn't talk much with Asma Fatima. Only me. For Asma Fatima puts him back into his place quick.

"Don't you know, *shauhar*? Everything turns into nothing. Even motherlands are taken away. Much less, mothers are abandoned," she would say. Then, using her few words she would whisper in my ear, "He left his mother to fight for the enemy. He knows nothing about loyalty," and we both prayed for Ali to not hear that. Ali would then threaten to rip another kid out of her belly. It was too much. Even in my line of work. I was blind, yes. Just not blind enough to not see suffering. Not just yet.

Asma Fatima

The baby was fed and burped. Asma Fatima's boobs were still working well. Even after the staple diet of air and water for breakfast, we had made it to another day. The niqab still doesn't leave her body. Ali on the other hand has little social manners left to him. Every morning, when the sun sets ablaze, he strips to his underwear and invites me to this little oasis he has found. Asma Fatima warned him that it was a mirage. This didn't help the poor woman's case. He bagged up the little belongings the poor lady had and set it on fire. Now we had another burning thing amongst the party lot. To this the baby turned and decided it liked my lap and my ugly severed eye more than anything else in this little, wretched world.

When done with his ritual bath, Ali would return with sand in his hands and rub it all over his feet. "To ward off the impurity!" He tells me, before he settles next to me under the piece of tarpaulin.

"Zubaida, how about I call you Tuheena?" He asked, and to this I used what I learnt from Asma Fatima. I didn't use my words.

"You would be as special if I called you by my lover's name," he craned his neck, and his sand laced finger moved against my neck. Asma Fatima sat helpless. The knife in her hand worked seamlessly against the flesh of a sorry bird.

The baby cried in my stead. The retortion was obvious. Lovers weren't found after they were lost. Ali won't be an exception. Not even with his stellar luck. "I am not your lover, Ali," I tell him and his pale blue eyes threaten to fall off. Just like mine. But they don't. Instead, he rests another hand on my thigh. My cry for help is a solitary glance at Asma Fatima. "Don't you have anything to say to him?" I said at last. But it was enough. Asma Fatima rose to her feet. The baby was taken away, and then she looked at me for one long minute. Then her feet moved. Away from the tarpaulin she went. The crows followed her closely. Their song chased away the light. Ali was too close. I was no longer Zubaida. I was Tuheena.

Twenty-nine years. That's how long I had waited. But it wasn't for Ali's undoing. The earless man whose coarse fingers grazed my skin wasn't my lover. The baby's father. That's what Ali should always be. So, when his fingers slipped around the hem of my cotton pants and tugged them down there was little I could do.

I would have used a "No. I don't want to," but a man who was used to people taking things away from him wasn't really up for a debate when it came to taking what he wanted for himself. Then went Ali's underwear and even in his naked spectacle all I could think of was the turkey. So, when Ali came in just at the right distance, I grabbed the solitary shrapnel Asma Fatima had saved from before. It wasn't too much. But just enough to let Ali know that there was no use of reproducing in no man's land. His severed meat set against the hot sand, coating it in its warmth. Jets of blood splayed out, running down his thighs. At that moment, there was more in common between Ali and Asma Fatima.

His knees bunched down, as his body slacked. His severed side of the head stuck down to the sand. His eyes turned lifeless. Ali was no longer a man. I rejoiced in it a little. But then, Ali stopped breathing. The crows closed in on him. They didn't touch the severed length. Only his eyes. They took away from him the most beautiful set of pearls he had owned. All ocean blue, all dead.

I sat in the middle of the Crow's feast as the sun burnt against my skin. I awaited Asma Fatima to return. And when she did, she only left the baby to join her husband. The crows didn't touch her. She seemed more alive than any of us. Or perhaps, she had mastered death in one lifetime. The baby stuck its head on my boob, sucking it for an eternity. Nothing came. And then it cried. Only cold winds blew when the baby cried. That's how we got to a new home.

Dua

The baby has a name now. Despite the fact that I don't know whether it's a boy or girl, I have decided to name it Dua. It was Asma Fatima who had introduced the word to me, while we were still deep in the clutches of the war. You bring your hands together, and then whisper a few words to the lord. This was called a dua. When you make a dua, it has the potential of being accepted by God.

"Allah, always accepts a selfless Dua," she would say. It was only fair that the child be named after something that sounds like a prayer. It was one of the few things that had made sure that we got out of the camp. There was no proof that the baby had existed on the planet. No identity. No parents. And no one to call its own. Isn't that how many prayers end up? In a pit of misery, never to be revoked? Luckily, Dua and I realised we needed each other. Despite the fact that all Dua did was cry, it was also the only thing that would make anyone take me with them.

When the men with guns first appeared on the horizon, it was a sign of the Universe. The crows seemed ecstatic. But I only had one eye to spare, and Dua's were pretty unused. You cannot take much from eyes that do not see.

"Get down on your knees, with your hands on the back," one of the two men with guns had said, pointing it to my head. Dua was still encased in my arms and it was impossible to leave her be on the ground. It was also the only thing that didn't look at me disgusted despite my deformed face. We were all hungry. All of us were waiting to get our hands on something that wasn't Turkey's head.

"The baby starts crying once you put it down. I don't have anything on me," I said, and one of them proceeded to snatch the baby from me. So I was on my knees, with my hands on my back. Dua, a little traitor that beamed innocence, didn't even cry at the loss of contact. The men who held it caressed its cheeks. But Dua remained unmoved.

"The baby's out cold," the man said, and something close to a sense of loss crept in for the very first time.

"Can you feel its pulse?" The man barks, and then they feel for its pulse. "It's there. But weak. This baby needs to be fed," he shouts back. Meanwhile, the other of the two touches me everywhere (even in the impossible places) to assess for anything that can cause harm. And at the end of it, they realised it was my clothes. I had to get rid of them. They replaced it with what seemed like a piece of curtain. It wrapped around me like a toga. I am a Bedouin now.

"We don't have enough space for another. Lose one of them," one of the men says, after we walked for what seemed like forever. Asma Fatima's turkey head didn't seem so bad now. Even with its undercooked meat and contempt for spice. Ali's coarse fingers didn't seem as hideous. Sweat laced my back, running down my spine. The distorted eye had begun to smell. The pain had shot up.

"You-"

An Eternity of Nothing

They nudged me down with the back of the gun and had me bend over in the sand. Its grains softly settled against my cheek. The tattered bandage that Ali had wound around my eye had come undone. I heard the rip of the fabric, as they exposed my behind to the sun.

"She's still fresh down here. Like a flower. Do you have a rubber?" One of them asks. Then their weight subdues me. Their knee digs into my spine. My body aches. Sweat shines off my palms. I stay there in a prostate as I feel the stretch of my folds. They were not like Ali. They were worse. They pushed in me and the sand under my body drifted and drifted, consuming me within the Earth. Baby Dua seemed to have known what I felt like. So, it cried in my stead again.

When both of them were done, they got up and pulled my head out of the sand. Their faces were red. That's all I know about their faces. Baby Dua's cries had made them reconsider.

"She's tight. Almost like a virgin. Maybe we should kill the baby," one of them says.

"Very well then," they proceeded to put the baby down in the sand. The easiest way for them to kill it was to neglect its existence. Maybe I had named the baby wrong. Like most Duas, the baby ended up in the most desolate ditch in the world, neglected, and left to die.

An Eternity of Nothing

I had killed the men when I got the chance. The war consumed me out, and it didn't feel different to see blood everywhere. It had its own allure, its own grotesque beauty. The cold undoing of life against all its own struggles.

It was almost a serendipity. Almost. The two men had left me for dead as I bled between my thighs. It was as if the stars had aligned. The last traces of energy curled up in my fist. I got a hold of the gun. Still loaded. Then emptied it. Their screams rolled out into the night and the moon arched its back between the clouds. I crawled to the little tent. Mongered on the little cans of food. I didn't dare wear their clothes. They were too tarnished. Too impure. I cut a cloth off the tarpaulin.

For an hour I rested with my blood-stuck locks. There was little water around here. Too little for me. Or for the baby. I traced my steps back into the desert in search of the little traitor. Though now, we were both equals. Dua and I, were equally betrayed and abandoned.

I had forgotten to ask Asma Fatima how one gets their prayer back. I wasn't a religious person. It never dawned on me the need to pray. However, I did believe there was some sort of immaculate power within names. A cryptic sermon that had the power to manifest. So, when my throat bobbed with the baby's name and my legs began to ache, I realised that faith wasn't my field of excellence.

My body slumped halfway back. There was no trace of Dua. The crows had disappeared. Nothing was burning. The crying of night had come to an end. The dawn rose. I crawled my way through the sand, acutely aware of the death that crawled through my eye. Asma Fatima's cold face followed my thoughts.

The desert was cold. The piece of tarpaulin that I wrapped around me was barely doing its job. All I wanted was to get to Dua. We could use the phone then. The phone that could take us out of the country. I saw the men talk about more people coming in today. They were going to take the refugees to the camp. If I made it to Dua, I could save us both.

But the sharp ringing of death throbbed in my pulse. Images of a dead baby haunted my head. I crept back into the cold sand. My knees stay buried in it. I turned to my back. My bleeding thighs parted to watch the brightest star shine in the sky. The Sun. This was peace. And peace meant death.

If I close my eyes now, I would know exactly how it felt like to be at home. The soft face of my mother and my father's sharp nose. The smell of fish soup and kimbap in my bedroom. There were only three of us. Mom, dad, and I. Then for some reason I had to dream big. And then, I had to grow out of my dream. That led me to another sad dream. Life.

The thought wasn't that dreary then. It was just a new home. A new place to live in. I worried I would get too comfortable with the thought of not leaving. And now there was no way for me to go back.

When they brought us all to camps, I thought this was when we got on the ship and never looked back. Two of my homes were in conflict. But there isn't much that can be done with how the wars end. Not the ones on the outside. Not the ones on the inside.

Then I met Asma Fatima, who had the biggest belly. And her husband, who had the most useless words. Then I left their baby to die in the cold. And in remorse here I laid.

Our dreams had led us to war. And war had brought us closer to life, and then to death. Sadly, death was the most forgiving of them all. Sadly, death was all that was left. I pictured the baby's face who I named as a prayer. I revelled in the truth that the prayer might have come to an end. The spirits of Asma Fatima and Ali parting ways, no longer hurting each other in death. In death, none of my homes were in conflict. There was a never-ending peace. An eternity of nothing. This was a better dream.

About the Author

Shanaya Stephens

Shanaya Stephens is an aspiring young adult and teen fiction writer from Vadodara, Gujarat, India. She is author of many poetry collections.

She is a Wattpad writer, and writes under the username-pea0buttersandwich. Her writings are deeply influenced by slam word artist, and renowned poet - Andrea Gibson, and Neil Hilborn. She is the recipient of Gold Award in Queen's Commonwealth Essay Competition (2022) in Senior Category. She also emerged as the winner of 'Christmas Contest 2.0' organised by the internationally acclaimed, GOI recognised Inkzoid Foundation and received an honourable mention in 'Inkzoid Book Of Records' for her feat.

Instagram: @shanaya_stephens_,

@pea0buttersandwich

Email: *stephensshanaya@gmail.com*

Other Titles by the Author

Vagabond
Love Gospel Be Thy, Queen
Modern Aphrodite
Small Things
Romantica
Sad for the sake of love
The Sandbox
Existential Crisis
The Complete Collection of Poems by Shanaya Stephens
The Bucketlist
The Dichotomy of Letting Go
Daddy Issues of a Dirty Dead, Depressed, Daughter
Cherry Fetish
Table For One
Butterflies, When They Die
The HOE Code
Strangers On The Internet
The Sans American Chutney Show
Now That We Are All Mad
Shun

www.ingramcontent.com/pod-product-compliance
Lightning Source LLC
LaVergne TN
LVHW041601070526
838199LV00046B/2081